Anatomy
of a Killer
Look Inside a Great White Shark
by David George Gordon

Build Your Own Model of
Carcharodon Carcharias

Anatomy of a Killer
Copyright becker&mayer! 2005
Published by Tangerine Press
An imprint of Scholastic Inc.
557 Broadway, New York, NY 10012
All rights reserved.

Produced by becker&mayer!, Ltd.
11010 Northup Way
Bellevue, WA 98004
www.beckermayer.com

If you have questions or comments about this product, send email to
infobm@beckermayer.com.
All rights reserved.

Anatomy of a Killer is part of the Look Inside a Great White Shark kit.
Not to be sold separately.

Edited by Don Roff
Art directed by Andrew Hess
Illustrated by Davide Bonadonna
Product design by Chris Tanner
Product photos by Keith Megay
Production management by Jennifer Marx

Image Credits
Book Cover Photo © Amos Nachoum/CORBIS
Page 11: Sawfish © Jay A. Stephenson Jr., used with permission.
Page 21: Great white shark © Oliver Damitz, used with permission.
Page 22: Shark jaws © Cleveland Museum of Natural History, used with
permission.
Page 27: "Flying" shark © Laurence Myriem BRAM, used with permission.

Every effort has been made to correctly attribute all the material reproduced in
this book. We will be happy to correct any errors in future editions.

Printed, manufactured, and assembled in China.
10 9 8 7 6 5 4 3 2 1
0-439-77755-0
04370

CONTENTS

What is a Great White Shark?

A NATURAL-BORN KILLER IS ON THE PROWL . . .

This passionless predator leaves his mark —a jagged, circular scar—on buoys and surfboards and, sometimes, on human flesh. His distinctive profile is all too familiar among sailors, scuba divers, and swimmers.

Beware of the Great White Shark

This book will give you a rare look inside the ocean's top predator. Once you've read it, you will know exactly what makes a great white shark tick. And you—will be well prepared to build your own lifelike replica of this awesome animal, one body part at a time.

Great White Sharks: The Basics

What is it about the great white shark, one of 350 living shark species, that strikes fear in our hearts?

Could it be the great white's huge, muscular body or massive tooth-lined jaws? Or perhaps it is the cold, unblinking eyes of this beast? Whatever the reason, one glimpse of the ocean's top predator is enough to tell us that danger is cruising nearby.

FACT!

Before *Star Wars*, the movie *Jaws* was Hollywood's all-time top moneymaker. The first of three *Jaws* movies cost $8 million to make and raked in about $260 million at the box office.

The longest confirmed great white shark is 19 1/2 feet. To you landlubbers, that's a little bit bigger than a minivan. People have filed fairly reliable reports of much larger specimens. More than one fisherman has claimed to have landed a 21-foot great white. Another says he tried but failed to capture a whopping 25-footer—the proverbial "one that got away."

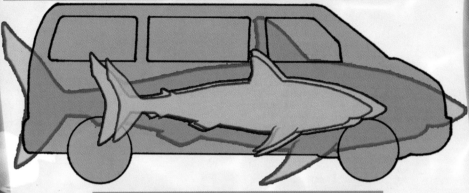

Standard minivan: 18 feet (5 ½ meters)

Longest confirmed great white shark: 19 ½ feet (6 meters)

Female great white shark: 11 feet (3 ⅓ meters)

Male great white shark: 10 feet (3 meters)

Female great whites are generally larger than males. Adults can weigh more than 2 1/4 tons—the same weight as 30 adult men.

Great white sharks swim without fear in all the world's oceans. The only enemies of adult great whites are killer (or orca) whales and any sharks that are bigger than them. Like all sharks, great whites are exclusively meat-eaters. They feed mostly on living creatures but will occasionally eat dead animals, if they find them.

Unfortunately for us, the live food of great white sharks includes human beings. Great whites are responsible for more fatal attacks on humans than any other species of shark. Those people who are not killed outright are often injured for life. Yes, we have good reasons for fearing these sharks.

Although they may frighten us, great white sharks are also sources of great fascination for most people. Their ancestors first appeared in our seas many millions of years ago, long before dinosaurs walked the earth.

Great White Shark Attacks

First, the good news. You are 52 times more likely to be bitten by a hamster than a shark. Now the bad news—a hamster can't bite you in half like a large great white shark can.

Most Common Shark Species in Attacks (167 cases)

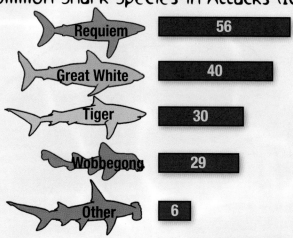

Requiem	56
Great White	40
Tiger	30
Wobbegong	29
Other	6

Great whites are responsible for about one-fourth of all reported shark attacks on humans. The record for great-white-related mayhem belongs to the now-famous Matawan, New Jersey man-eater. Over a 10-day period in July 1916, this hungry shark killed four people and seriously injured a fifth before it was captured by a local fisherman. Or so the story goes. Some scientists have questioned whether this was the work of a single shark or several animals operating off the same stretch of coast.

FACT!
You are 30 times more likely to be killed by a falling coconut than by a shark.

While we might call them man-eaters, there's plenty of evidence to suggest that great whites may be best described as "man-biters." In more than half of all known great white shark attacks on swimmers, the attackers took only one bite and then swam away.

FACT!
Those single nips may be the shark's way of saying "Beat it. This is my side of the street." Or they could mean that people just don't taste so good compared to a seal or a fish.

Areas Where Sharks Attacked Humans

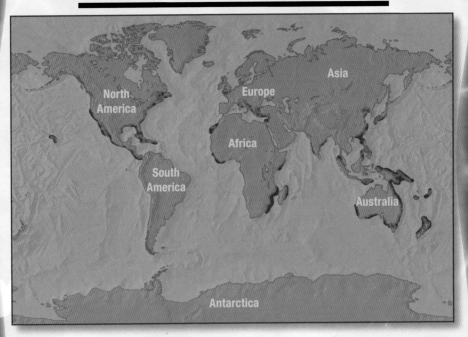

Here are a few ways to avoid coming face-to-face with a great white:

➤ Don't swim or wade in the sea at dawn, dusk, and night, when the sharks move in closer to shore.

➤ Pay heed to warning signs or radio reports of beaches where great whites have been seen. The sharks tend to stick around in one area, especially if the pickings are good.

➤ Stick to beaches with lifeguards, who can do double duty as great white watchers.

➤ Always swim with a partner.

➤ Avoid beaches near seal rookeries or haul-outs. Great whites often patrol these spots, waiting to nab an unsuspecting pup or adult seal. You wouldn't want to be mistaken for one of those!

FACT!

Stay out of the water if you're bleeding from an open wound. It doesn't pay to advertise!

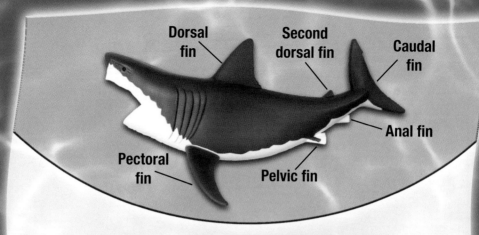

Dorsal fin

Second dorsal fin

Caudal fin

Anal fin

Pectoral fin

Pelvic fin

THE SCRATCHIEST SKIN

The sleek, streamlined body of a great white shark is covered with a layer of prickly skin. Look close enough (if you can) and you'll see hundreds of thousands of tiny points called dermal denticles or "skin-teeth" dotting the skin.

The streamlined denticles of great white sharks reduce drag and help the shark slip quietly through the water.

The denticles are made of calcium—just like your teeth—hence their name. The cusp of each denticle points backward toward the shark's tail. That's why the great white's skin feels smooth if stroked from head to tail, but rough if stroked in the other direction.

Great white shark denticles have three ridges on their upper surfaces. The ridges taper off and meet at the denticle's rear-facing edge. It may be hard to imagine, but these ridges give the shark extra speed in the water, much like the dimples on a golf ball help the ball shoot through the air.

Remote Contact

Great white sharks have something called a *lateral line system*, which is a series of pores that runs the length of the shark's body. Beneath the pores are cells with tiny hairs. By responding to water pressure and vibrations, this "remote contact" system gives the shark tactile clues regarding its environment. It can even tell the relative position of other sharks that swim nearby.

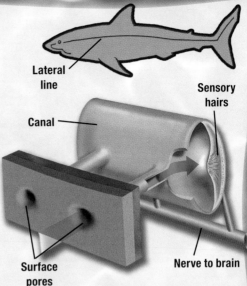

Lateral line

Canal

Surface pores

Sensory hairs

Nerve to brain

Great white sharks have one more trick to their skin: countershading. The shark's belly is light-colored and blends with the sunlit surface waters when glimpsed from below. Its back is a dark bluish gray tone, to match the colors of the shadowy sea floor. Great whites aren't the only ones to use this trick. Penguins, saltwater and freshwater fish—and even fighter planes—use countershading to their advantage.

Emperor penquins

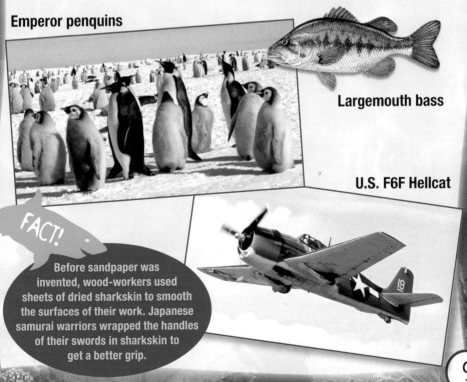

Largemouth bass

U.S. F6F Hellcat

FACT!

Before sandpaper was invented, wood-workers used sheets of dried sharkskin to smooth the surfaces of their work. Japanese samurai warriors wrapped the handles of their swords in sharkskin to get a better grip.

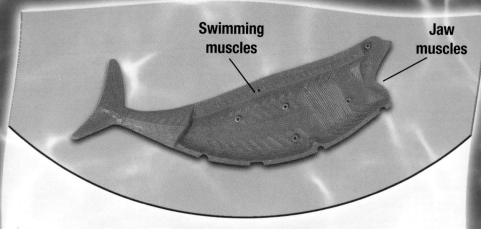

Swimming muscles

Jaw muscles

MUSCLE MANIA

A great white shark is a muscle-bound brute. The entire rear half of its body is wrapped in thick bands of skeletal muscle to power the shark's flexible tail.

The zigzag bands of tail muscles in the great white shark allow the tail and body to flex from side to side.

With all that power behind it, a great white can zoom through the water at peak speeds of 35 miles per hour (56 kilometers per hour). That's faster than an Olympic swimmer—and about five times faster than you could ever go. Scientists tracked one great white as it swam from California to Hawaii, covering 2,400 miles (3862 kilometers) in only 40 days. In False Bay, South Africa, great whites are often seen leaping out of the water and "flying" through the air in pursuit of Cape fur seals.

Other bands of muscle are attached to the great white's gills, pectoral fins and, of course, those dangerous snapping jaws.

It Takes Two

Muscles cannot push but can only pull. So to move the great white's tail from side to side, the muscles must be arranged in pairs. One muscle pulls the tail in one direction while the other relaxes and "goes along for the ride." Then the roles are reversed. Now the other muscle pulls, while its partner relaxes. These are called *antagonistic muscles*.

Great white sharks use their muscles to make small adjustments to their fins or bodies while gliding through the water, and for short bursts of speed. An attacking great white may suddenly turn and glide away if its muscles become tuckered out.

FACT!

Even though they work together to help the shark swim, they call those muscles "antagonistic."

FACT!

Shark meat is really shark muscle. In South Korea, great white shark meat sometimes sells for 15 US dollars a pound!

There's a growing market for shark meat. Shark steaks are popular items on many restaurant menus. In Britain, the "fish" in fish 'n' chips is often dogfish shark meat. Shark fins are also treasured in an Asian delicacy, shark-fin soup.

Overfishing may be causing some sharks to disappear from the world's oceans. Several species of sharks and related fish, including sawfish, whale sharks, basking sharks, and the great white, are endangered. This means they have a very high risk of becoming extinct in the near future.

Basking shark

Sawfish

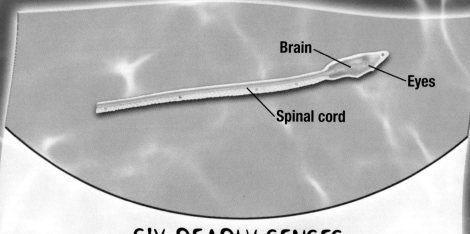

Brain

Eyes

Spinal cord

SIX DEADLY SENSES

While swimming, great white sharks gather an assortment of sensory clues about the watery world around them. In addition to the usual five senses—sight, scent, hearing, taste, and touch—great white sharks have an electrical sense, *electrosense*, that lets them know if any other animals are nearby. Some scientists believe that this sixth sense also helps the great white navigate. The electrical sense could be useful for "reading" the earth's magnetic fields. Since there are no highway signs underwater, that extra info might keep the great white from getting lost.

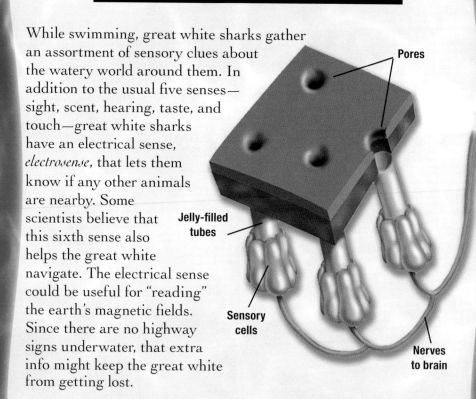

Pores

Jelly-filled tubes

Sensory cells

Nerves to brain

Scattered among the denticles—especially around the head—are thousands of small holes. These pores are the surface openings to long, jelly-filled tubes. The tubes lead to special sensory organs (called *ampullae of Lorenzini*), which pick up on the very weak electric currents that flow from all living things. This helps the great white home in on live food, even if it is buried in the sandy seafloor.

If the ocean is murky, great whites cannot see very far underwater. That doesn't stop them from getting a good look-see. Great whites can lower a protective shield over each eye. The shields come down right before the shark strikes, protecting these delicate sense organs from getting scratched.

Nictitating membranes protect the eyes of attacking sharks.

Nictitating membrane

Hear, Hear!

Yes, great white sharks have ears. They are not big and obvious, though. You can't see them from the outside. Still, they exist as two sensors in the skull. These can pick up the splashing noises of a wounded seal or fish. To the great white, those sounds mean "Dinner is served."

Fluid-filled tubes detect sounds and regulate balance.

Compared to other sharks, the great white has a fairly large, well-developed brain. Still, it is puny compared to our own brain. For example, the brain of a 950-pound (431 kilograms) great white weighs only 1.2 ounces (34 grams). This pencils out to less than one hundredth of one percent of the shark's total body weight. By comparison, the brain of an average-sized adult human weighs about 48 ounces (1 $\frac{1}{3}$ kilogram)—and is nearly two percent of a person's body weight. In other words, humans have more than 200 times more brain matter for each pound of body weight.

FACT!

Great whites are the only sharks that can raise their heads out of the water. That's how they take a peek at a seal or anything else they want to munch on.

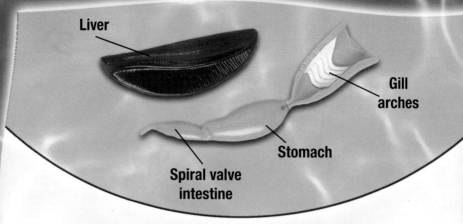

Liver

Gill arches

Stomach

Spiral valve intestine

AL DENTE (TO THE TEETH)

Great white sharks eat seals, sea lions, porpoises, dolphins, sea turtles, sea gulls, lobsters, crabs, fish of all shapes and sizes—and the occasional human being.

Sharks seem to swallow practically everything. An odd assortment of items, from tin buckets and lobster traps to a cuckoo clock, a rubber tire and a knight's shining armor have been retrieved from the stomachs of great whites.

FACT!

Since the ocean is a vast place, the chances of meeting a tasty seal or a porpoise in the middle of the sea are... well... slim.

The great white's spiral valve helps the shark get the most from its meals. The inside of this compact organ looks like a corkscrew or a spiral staircase. Partially digested food is broken down further by juices inside the spiral valve.

Any waste material is then pumped from the *spiral valve* into the great white's *cloaca*—sort of a waiting room where the shark's genital and urinary ducts meet. From there, the waste enters the water surrounding the shark. No muss, no fuss.

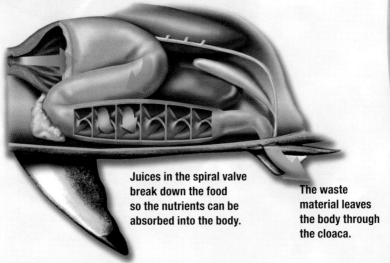

Partially digested food moves from the stomach to the spiral valve intestine.

Juices in the spiral valve break down the food so the nutrients can be absorbed into the body.

The waste material leaves the body through the cloaca.

Living Large with a Large Liver

The shark's twin-lobed liver fills any extra space inside a great white. It stores vitamins and removes impurities from the bloodstream. Because this enormous organ is rich in oil, it is actually lighter than the water the shark swims in. As such, it helps keep the shark from sinking to the bottom of the sea.

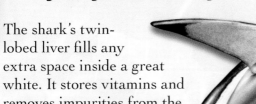

The enormous, oil-filled liver helps keep the shark afloat. The liver also helps the shark turn food into energy.

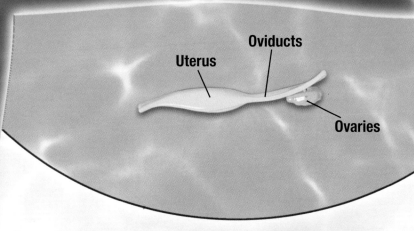

Uterus

Oviducts

Ovaries

A SHARK IS BORN

Q: What do 19-foot-long great whites and inch-long guppies have in common?
A: Both fish carry their babies in their bellies until they are born.

Great white sharks do not lay eggs like most other fish. Their eggs are fertilized internally, just like other sharks' eggs. However, instead of laying their fertilized eggs, female great whites keep them inside. Here, the eggs slowly mature into five-foot-long babies, called pups.

When a female great white is 10 or 12 years old, she may be ready to bear her first litter of pups. An adult male great white will wrap his body around hers. Then he inserts one of his paired genitals, called a *clasper*, into the female's genital opening, called a *vent*. Sperm flows from the clasper into the egg tubes, or *oviducts*, to fertilize the great white shark eggs. The entire process takes about half an hour.

Shark Ancestors

Covering a period of 450 million years, the reign of sharks has been three times longer than that of the dinosaurs—and 100 times longer than our own! There were sharks in our oceans long before the first creatures crawled onto land, and even before the earliest insects took to the sky. The fact that sharks are still thriving today proves how good they are at surviving and adapting.

Some ancient sharks looked similar to the present-day frilled shark.

No Room in This Womb

It takes about 14 months before the pups are ready to be born. As many as 17 of these baby sharks spend that time crammed in their mother's womb. While they are waiting, the pups sometimes snack on any unfertilized eggs in the womb. Some people think the hungriest pups may also dine on each other.

When the pups are ready to be born, they swim out of their mother's belly and into the open sea. They eat fish, squid, and anything else they can catch. They must keep an eye out for bigger sharks, which may view the pups as live food instead of close kin.

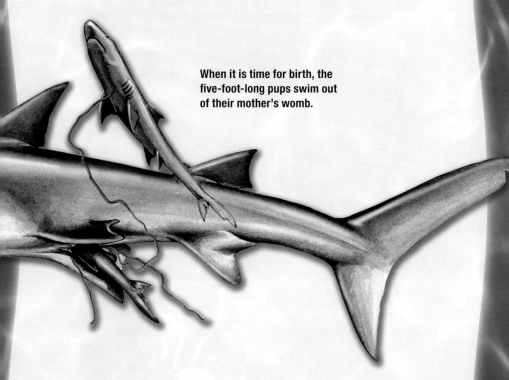

When it is time for birth, the five-foot-long pups swim out of their mother's womb.

Great whites are slow-growing creatures, gaining only a few inches in length for each year of life. There are many hidden dangers in the sea, and as feisty as they may be, many pups do not reach adulthood. For these reasons, some people think great white sharks are extra sensitive to threats posed by humankind. (See page 25 to learn more about shark conservation.)

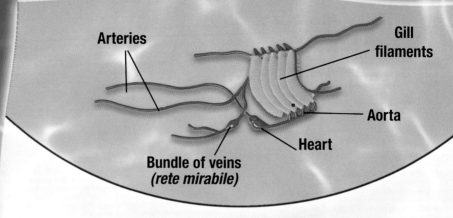

Arteries

Gill filaments

Aorta

Heart

Bundle of veins
(*rete mirabile*)

THRILLS AND GILLS

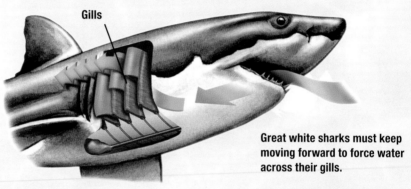

Gills

Great white sharks must keep moving forward to force water across their gills.

Great white sharks have gills, just like other fish. These feathery features grab the oxygen in seawater and pass it to small tubes called *capillaries*. The capillaries feed the oxygen-rich blood to bigger tubes, called *arteries*, which lead to the heart.

The heart pumps the blood into other arteries and capillaries throughout the shark's body. The shark's body cells use up the oxygen and release carbon dioxide back into the blood.

This blood flows through a series of veins leading back to the gills. The gills release the carbon dioxide back into the seawater.

That may sound complicated, but the same thing happens inside of us. We have lungs instead of gills, though.

FACT!

Lungs work better when you live on land.

Mouth-Breathers

Great white sharks are always on the move. If they had to stop, they would strangle and die. Here's why.

Most fish have special muscles for pumping water through their gills. If you watch a fish closely, you can see it open and close its mouth. This gulping movement helps the fish push water back to the gills.

Great white sharks don't have those muscles. They don't gulp like other fish, either. Instead, they swim with their mouths open. This forces seawater to flow through their gills and out through the gill slits. It's a neat trick.

Unlike most fish, the blood of a great white is warmer than the water the shark swims in. That's because the shark's veins and arteries are bundled together to hold in heat. This can raise the shark's body temperature by as much as 27 degrees Fahrenheit (3 degrees Celcius). "Hot-blooded" sharks can swim faster and digest their meals more quickly. That's handy for a killer that has to keep moving to survive.

Special bundles of veins help hot-blooded sharks conserve their body heat.

In cold-blooded sharks, heat is quickly lost as it travels through the fish's body.

Vertebral column

BONELESS BODS

Unlike people—or, for that matter, most fish—great white sharks have no bones in their bodies. Sharks belong to the group of fish called *elasmobranchs* (i-LAZ-muh-branks). The skeletons of elasmobranchs are made of *cartilage*—the material that gives shape to our ears and noses. Bone skeletons are rigid, but cartilage skeletons are flexible like rubber. Elasmobranchs are also called *cartilaginous* fish.

This doesn't mean that sharks are all soft and squishy. The cartilage is flexible but it is also rigid. After all, those powerful antagonistic muscles must attach themselves to something. The main site of attachment is the shark's *vertebral column*. This long rod runs the length of the shark's back. It is really a series of thick disks, strung like beads on the great white's spinal cord. The disks give the shark greater flexibility and allow it to swish its tail with ease.

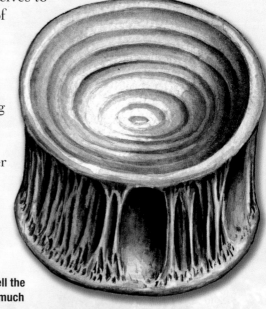

Viewed from the front, each vertebral disk shows a pattern of circular growth rings. By carefully counting the rings, scientists can tell the age of the shark that made them—much like counting the rings of a tree.

The great white's skull is basically a brain box, and not a very big one at that. It is called the *cranium* and has sockets on its sides for the eyes. The upper jaw is connected to the cranium.

Broad bands of cartilage give the gills and gill slits their shapes. These are called *gill arches*. Great whites have five pairs of gill arches and gill slits. Other types of sharks have six or seven pairs of arches and slits.

FACT!

Wanna know how old a shark is? Just count the growth rings in its vertebral disks. Every year a shark gets a new ring… just like the rings on a tree. You'd have to cut one open, though, to see its rings.

Gill slits

Gill arches

FACT!

Unlike bone, cartilage has no blood vessels running through it. Maybe blood vessels cost extra?

FACT!

A great white's heart is a tube that acts like a pump. It sucks in blood from the veins and pumps it into the arteries.

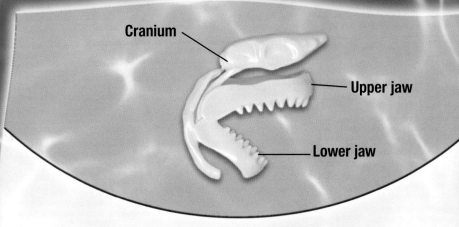

Cranium

Upper jaw

Lower jaw

THE BIG BITE

The great white's jaws are lined with dozens of razor-sharp teeth. Behind the first row of teeth are several rows of replacements.

Whenever a great white shark loses a front tooth, one of the spares moves forward into position. Great whites lose and replace thousands of teeth during their lifetimes. Other sharks lose their teeth at about the same rate. That may be one reason why fossilized teeth from ancient sharks are so easy to find.

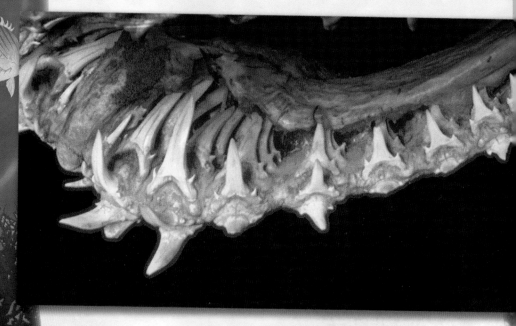

A shark's rotating teeth.

FACT!

Because larger sharks, especially great whites, are so rare, this makes big teeth difficult to find—and extremely valuable!

The great white's top teeth are triangular. Their sides have small ridges for sawing, just like the blade of a steak knife. One of these whopper-sized choppers can be two-and-a-half inches long. That's nearly six times the size of your biggest tooth.

A great white's lower teeth are more pointed. They are designed for piercing animal flesh and for holding it in place while the upper teeth do their job.

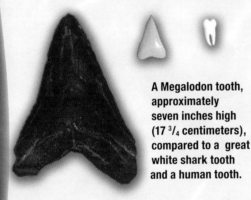

A Megalodon tooth, approximately seven inches high (17 ³/₄ centimeters), compared to a great white shark tooth and a human tooth.

Even these giant-sized teeth are quite puny compared to those of the great white's ancient relative, *Megalodon*. Teeth from this big-mouthed beast were seven inches long.

Based on the size of its teeth, scientists think Megalodon was bigger than the king of dinosaurs, *Tyrannosaurus rex*. The prehistoric shark was about 50 feet (15 ¹/₄ meters) from its snout to the tip of its tail.

Crrrunch!

A great white shark's jaws are remarkably strong. They can chomp their way through a thick metal chain or steel cable. Imagine what a bite like that could do to a scuba diver's arm or leg. Let's hope you never find out!

Upper and lower jaws are only loosely attached to the skull. When a great white takes a bite, it tilts its head up and back, pushing both jaws forward. It strikes with the lower jaw first, and then slams the upper jaw downward, slicing with those super-sharp teeth. The shark shakes its head from side to side, ripping off a huge hunk of flesh.

Great White Friends and Foes

Hammerheads, dogfish, and several other types of sharks may gather in large numbers while feeding or during breeding seasons. However, great white sharks are loners, traveling solo for most of their lives. Aside from killer whales, pods of dolphins, and larger-sized great whites, they have no natural enemies, and, of course—they don't need help from others to capture and kill their prey.

Even solitary animals may have companions, whether they know it or not. Like all sharks, great whites carry parasites, both inside their bodies and attached to their outsides. These small *copepods* and worms seldom hinder a healthy shark. Rather, they often go unnoticed, feeding on small quantities of the shark's body fluids and tissue for weeks, months, and even years at a time.

Remora

Remora attached to shark.

Technically, *remoras* are not parasites. By attaching themselves to the bodies of great whites, these fish get free rides. The top of a remora's head looks like the sole of an athletic shoe. The "sole" acts like a suction cup. It is really a highly modified fin.

Pilot fish

Another great white companion is called a *pilot fish*. This relative of the tuna and mackerel can grow to two feet in length. Pilot fishes swim alongside or in front of large sharks, apparently to feed on parasites and any scraps of leftover meat. People once thought that pilot fish were leading, or "piloting," the sharks to food, hence their name.

Conclusion (Shark Conservation)

Nobody knows for sure how long great whites can live, although 20 to 25 years is a good guess. Because sharks are slow growing, they must be protected from overly eager fishermen. If too many immature sharks are caught and killed, the population may dwindle or disappear entirely from our planet's seas.

It is a fish-eat-fish world. As prey for other sharks, baby great whites are sources of protein. As predators, the adults help keep the numbers of prey species in proportion, ensuring a healthy balance between the eaters and the eaten. As scavengers, they help break down the bodies of dead animals, releasing much-needed vitamins and minerals into the ocean system.

Both California and South Africa have laws preventing the capture of great white sharks for food or for fun. Other states and nations are planning to pass similar rules.

Now that you have studied the wonders of sharkdom, you are probably ready to save the great white, too!

Great White Glossary

Ampullae of Lorenzini: Sensory organs found in the noses of certain marine animals, including the shark, which allows the detection of prey.

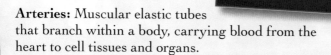

Antagonistic: A force that works against itself, like the antagonistic muscles that work inside in a shark.

Arteries: Muscular elastic tubes that branch within a body, carrying blood from the heart to cell tissues and organs.

Capillaries: Tiny blood vessels that allow the interchange of substances such as oxygen and carbon dioxide between blood and cell tissue.

Carcharodon Carcharias: The scientific name of a great white shark.

Cartilage: Tough, elastic, fibrous connective tissue that makes up the structure of a shark instead of bones.

Cartilaginous Fish: Marine animals made up primarily of cartilage. See *Elasmobranchs.*

Clasper: A rear extension of the pelvic fins of a male shark that aids in the transmission of sperm during reproduction.

Cloaca: The common cavity into which the intestinal, genital, and urinary tracts open in vertebrates like sharks and other fish.

Copepod: Small marine animals that have an elongated body and a forked tail.

Countershading: Protective coloration of a shark, typically with darker coloring of areas exposed to light and lighter coloring of areas that are normally shaded.

Cranium: The brain of an organism.

Dermal Denticles: Shark scales that have a tooth-like structure; literally meaning "tiny skin teeth."

Dorsal Fin: The main fin located on the back of fish and certain marine mammals.

Elasmobranchs: Fish characterized by a cartilaginous skeleton, such as sharks, rays, and skates.

Electrosense: A unique and highly specialized bioelectrical sensory system in sharks, scattered over the front of their heads. See *Ampullae of Lorenzini*.

Gills: The respiratory organ of most aquatic animals that breathe water to receive oxygen.

Lateral Line: In fish, a line of sensory organs along either side of the body, often marked by a distinct line of color.

Megalodon: A prehistoric shark estimated in length of up to 50 feet (16 meters) based on the fossilized teeth; literally meaning "giant tooth."

Nictitating Membrane: A transparent inner eyelid in birds, reptiles, and some mammals that closes to protect and moisten the eye. Also called third eyelid.

Oviduct: A tube which the eggs pass through from the ovary to the uterus or to the outside.

Pectoral Fin: Either of the anterior pair of fins attached to the pectoral girdle of fish, corresponding to the forelimbs of higher vertebrates.

Rete Mirabile: A vascular network that interrupts the continuity of an artery or vein, as in the liver.

Sperm: Reproductive fluid emitted from a male organism, such as a shark.

Uterus: A hollow organ in the pelvic cavity of the female shark, in which the fertilized egg implants and develops. Also called a womb.

Vertebral Column: The series of articulated vertebrae that extends from the cranium to the end of the tail; the spine.

Assembly Instructions

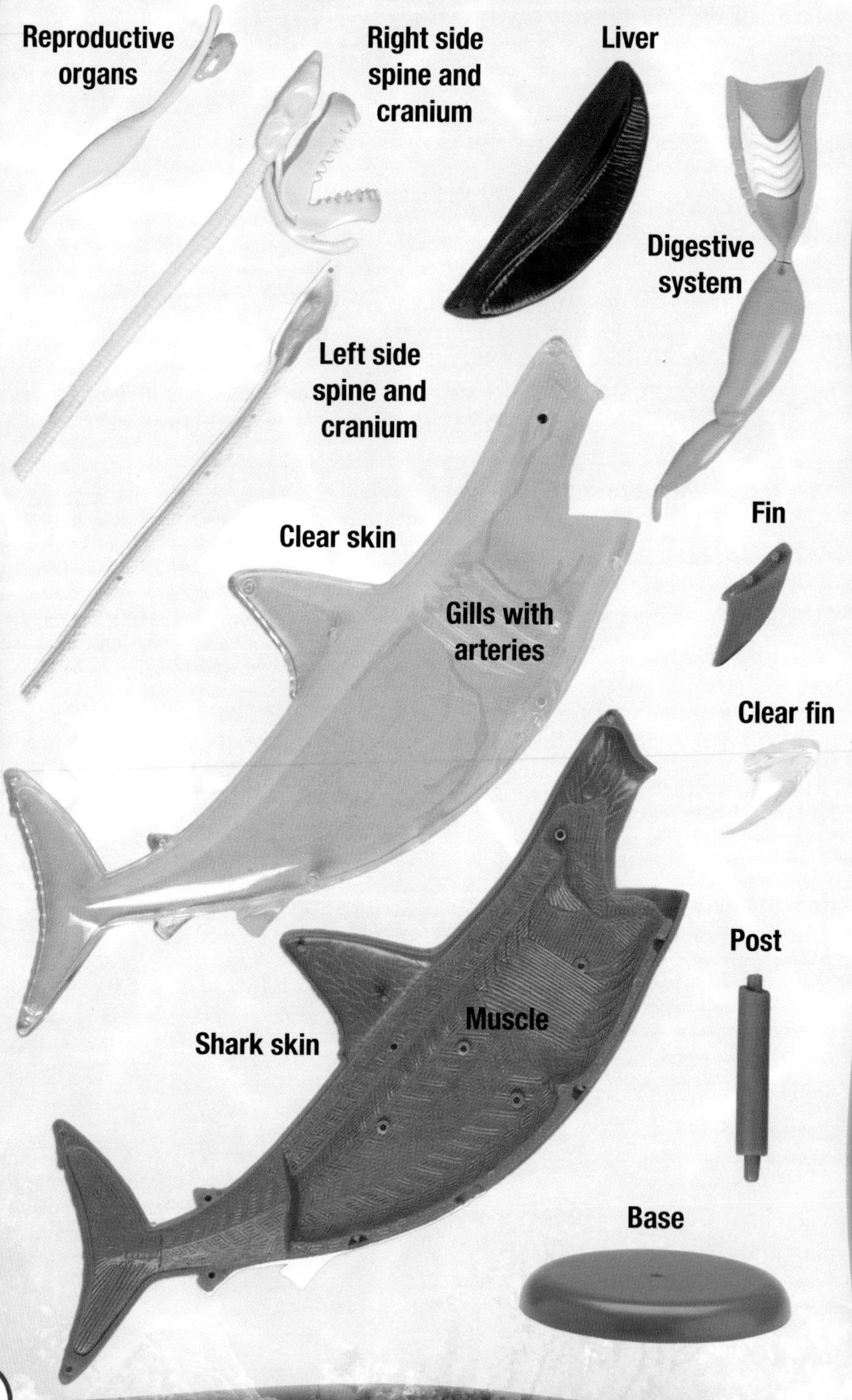

Reproductive organs

Right side spine and cranium

Liver

Digestive system

Left side spine and cranium

Clear skin

Gills with arteries

Fin

Clear fin

Post

Muscle

Shark skin

Base

Assembly Instructions

1. Ensure that the **muscle** is snapped into the **skin** (pre-assembled).

2. Attach the left side of the **spine and cranium** to the inside of the muscle.

3. Place the **liver** into the muscle (under spinal cord).

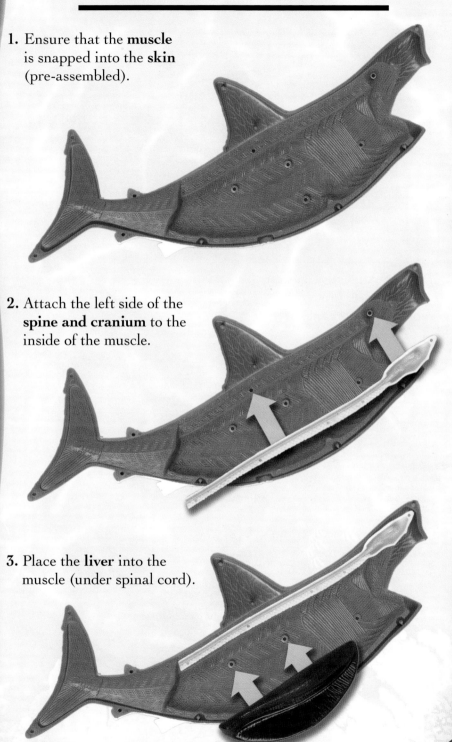

4. Attach the **reproductive organs** to the liver.

5. Place the **digestive system** on the muscle (under the reproductive organs).

6. Place the right side **spine and cranium** onto the already attached left side spine and cranium.

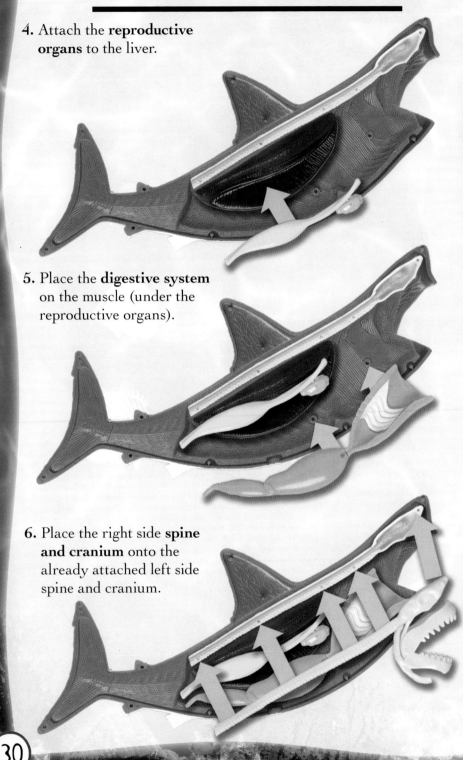

7. Ensure that the **gills with arteries** is snapped into the **shark skin** (pre-assembled).

8. Attach the right side of clear **shark skin** to the assembled shark left side.

9. Place the right clear **shark fin** onto the right side of shark skin.

Assembly Instructions

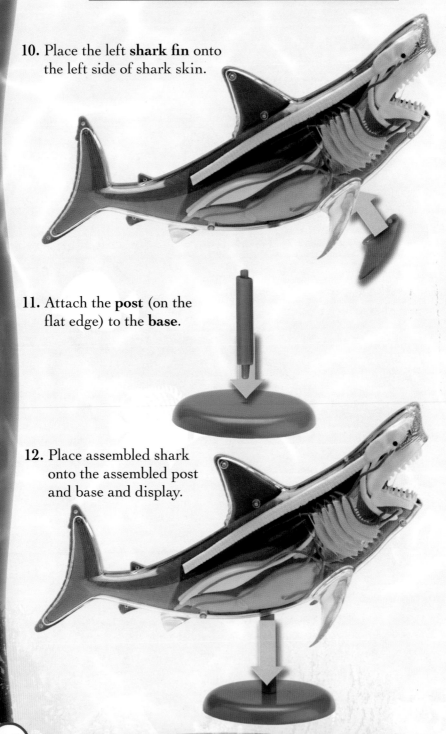

10. Place the left **shark fin** onto the left side of shark skin.

11. Attach the **post** (on the flat edge) to the **base**.

12. Place assembled shark onto the assembled post and base and display.